I0689856

Charles A. Sumner

**Oration**

Charles A. Sumner

**Oration**

ISBN/EAN: 9783744681056

Printed in Europe, USA, Canada, Australia, Japan

Cover: Foto ©Andreas Hilbeck / pixelio.de

More available books at **www.hansebooks.com**

BY

# CHARLES A. SUMNER,

Of San Francisco, California,

DELIVERED AT

## Great Barrington, Massachusetts,

ON

## JULY 4, 1861.

———— ◆ ————

SPRINGFIELD:
SAMUEL BOWLES & COMPANY, PRINTERS.
1861.

# CORRESPONDENCE.

CHARLES A. SUMNER, Esq.

My Dear Sir:—At the close of your eloquent and able address, delivered at the late Fourth of July in this town, the people with unanimous voice asked for its publication. As President of the day, it is my duty and pleasure to respectfully submit to you their desire, trusting that it will be compatible with your inclination, to gratify them.

Very Respectfully,

Your Ob't Serv't.

J. SEDGWICK.

Great Barrington. July 5, 1861.

JAMES SEDGWICK, Esq.

Dear Sir:—The Address, a desire by my old fellow townsmen for the publication of which you have communicated to me in flattering terms, was in affirmative reply to an invitation which afforded me less than four days time for preparation. With this fact understood by the reader, I am willing that it should pass into printed form, without revision or alteration.

Yours Truly,

CHARLES A. SUMNER.

Great Barrington, July 6, 1861.

BANCROFT LIBRARY

# ORATION.

Mr. President and Fellow Citizens:

Such are the demands of the Present upon our thoughts and feelings and practical energies, such the tendency of a large portion of the American mind to fritter away the auspicious hours for action in fruitless and demoralizing harangues, that we have the popular saying: It is no time for talk.

It is no time, fellow citizens, for characterless speech. That which is said, not belonging to the unimpeachable record of the past, unconnected with the issues immediately before us, outside of the probable emergencies of the future, involves in its delivery something worse than a waste of breath on the part of the speaker and of patience on the part of his audience. This is, indeed, not an hour for the display of that species of vegetable, compromise oratory which in our land is continually fed and nurtured into blossom on the mephitic vapors of morbid and temporary excitements.

But, surely, a little reflection will relieve us of confusion of ideas concerning the abuses of language at this juncture, and the decent, wholesome and necessary requirements for its use. With the severe education which we have all received within the past few months, there need be no lack of proper discrimination as to what compose the elements of manly and patriotic speech. Nor can I be mistaken in affirming—to me a very consoling reflection—neither great talents nor elaborate preparation are absolutely requisite to the fulfillment of such an appointment as I have been honored with on this occasion in a manner consistent with the just laws and limitations already intimated. In the peculiar vernacular of our commercial age and country, we may declare that the rules of " business " have laid hold of the terms of speech and, without any degrading or injurious effects, have forced the appetites of the people and the corresponding ambition and endeavors of those who are accustomed to comment upon passing events, to appeal to general sympathies, to invoke regard for enduring principles, in new, more pertinent and accomplishing channels. Then I shall very briefly occupy your attention, not with many chosen forms of words—for time has not been given me to prepare such, if I would—but at all moments in obedience to what I conceive to be the exact wish of the day.

This is the eighty-fifth anniversary of the Declaration of Independence. The day has been rendered familiar, from earliest childhood, to the vast majority of those here assembled by the recurrence with it of demonstrations of the order which we now witness. The record of events we celebrate has passed into so many forms of literature, is springing forth in so many conversations of our lives, that to present it now in specific rehearsal might seem a work of supererogation and impertinence. But a part of the humble though earnest endeavor of the hour ought not to be other than an attempt to freshen our recollections of the Past, in order that we may deepen our impressions of the danger, the privileges, the sublimity of the Present. And with the parallels and contrasts afforded by recent experiences, the task ought not to be difficult or wearisome.

Through trials and tribulations, which challenge for their representation all titles of pain and honor, our fathers secured for us this goodly heritage. It becomes us always to study the history of their labors and sufferings ; it is required of us to-day, that we give them especial thanks for their struggles in successful vindication of the inalienable rights of man. And to excite again, with stronger flame, this sentiment of gratitude in your hearts, we need but refer to the indisputable calendar of their generation. Every day of their battle is remembered; every soldier and statesman who rendered his country important service and honor, has a monument in our regard.

The story of the Revolution permits no eulogium. In its simple letter it shadows in vanity the praise of man. And let no one, however distinguished, however capable or felicitous in the employment of eulogistic phrase, in foolish conceit lift up his single taper to throw back light upon the brilliantly self-illuminated pages of our national history.

Eighty-five years ago to-day, the Declaration of Independence which asserted the equal right of all men to life, liberty and the pursuit of happiness, was given to the world. The bell which swung in the tower of the old Continental Congress Hall, in Philadelphia, proclaimed from its brazen throat the adoption of those immortal articles of political faith, and struck the key note of the anthem of a new Republic.

It is an observation which invariably attaches itself to a review of all great movements destined to secure permanent and blessed results, that their inception and their growth into systematic lines, is very gradual; that their originators and conductors approach their decisive actions, not only with unhurried steps, but with much of reluctance and unconsciousness. That which can be expressed in the description of mere impulse is far from revealing the might and majesty of their motives and deeds. A single though grievous insult may not provoke a wise man to wrath and strife. A series of injuries were long and patiently endured, and then humbly complained of, by our ancestors, before the idea of concerted rebellion and separation was entertained and developed. Their representations of grievances made to the authorities and the inhabitants of the mother country, were submitted for years in language of unmistakable subordination and affection; nay, with positive and oft-repeated declarations of a profound loyalty, which lent a more stinging sorrow to their burden of regret and supplication.

At the same time, it is worthy of our notice at this juncture in our domestic affairs, our Revolutionary sires made no concealment of whatever of intention they had respecting their course of action in resentment and for reparation. While they exhibited through years of oppression a scrupulous fidelity to the parent Government, continually and with unquestioned sincerity announcing their fidelity to the crown, an enlightened and candid Ministry could not have failed to understand the exact purpose of the Colonists in every movement of their remonstrance, up to the very date of the first battle of the Revolution. And the Rulers of Great Britain could only declare their surprise at the tidings of the encounter at Lexington, because blinded by a disposition of insolent and unpitying tyranny.

There were no robberies of the King's arsenals; no plundering of his magazines and warehouses; no insults were returned to the overbearing soldiery who for months lived virtually on the bounty of the Massachusetts Colonists, and who stalked with outrageous offence through the streets of Boston. No cry ascended from the Representatives of the Colony, that their soil was too sacred for the tread of an armed Briton; only, and ever, and with a stern calmness came the voice of remonstrance and pleading against "inequality in taxation and representation." And when they were forced to hostile measures, the people of Boston Bay extemporised themselves as Indian stevedores, and instead of stealing the cargo, rendered obnoxious by the unjust impost which had been placed upon it, they indignantly and contemptuously tumbled it into the sea.

It is not to be disputed that the war of the Revolution, as conducted by the American leaders, introduced a better, and what is worthy of the name of a moral code into the contentions of opposing armies. All through those times of trial, a profound respect for the constructive rights of the enemy, a fraternal sympathy with and care for the wounded and captured foe, a willingness to sacrifice all of temporary advantage for a fair contest, a regard amounting to delicate tenderness for the feelings of the discomfited chieftains were made as clearly and splendidly manifest as was the unconquerable determination to abide by the assertion of the principles of common freedom to the bitterest possible conclusion. In proof of this, speak out all the volumes of our history. And in exceeding shameful contrast stand the records of the deeds of those who have recently excited insurrection within the borders of the Republic which was so gloriously born—so magnanimously maintained unto a universally recognized and admired existence. Be .it ours, as true children of our Revolutionary sires, to continue the erection of the nobler monuments of civilized warfare.

But here we should not fail to remember that other fact, so significant and commendable at this time: whenever, according to the acknowledged discipline of war, the upholding of our cause demanded the execution of the extreme penalty of the law, not even a sentence or sanction by the christian Washington was wanting, though he blotted the death warrant which he signed with his tears; not even the brilliant talents and accomplishments, and the noble temper of an Andre, could shield a convicted spy from the doom which the world's custom had appointed as a consequence of his established guilt. Although we are not informed that the British ever perpetrated such dreadful and wanton cruelties upon their captives as have been inflicted by the rebels of this day and land upon defenceless men, women and children, suspected merely of immovable love for the Union, our generous fathers did not learn, as they certainly never cultivated and practiced, the transcendental art of detecting the vilest and most unscrupulous foes in the disguise of friends, to gently and hospitably retain their persons for a brief season and then release them on their word of honor.

Mr. Sumner spoke of other events which deserved to be cherished with emphasis this day.

He recounted the main and stirring incidents in the battle of Fort Moultrie, in Charleston harbor, in the latter part of June, 1776: calling to remembrance the fact that the brave commander of the American forces engaged in that contest, who had held his little Palmetto fort against a formidable fleet of British vessels, directed in their operations by experienced and skillful naval officers,—forcing the enemy to retire after a severe and protracted cannonade, with riddled hulls and terrible losses of men—on this day, eighty-five years ago, received the congratulations of his superior officers, and was informed that the spot which he had so gallantly and successfully defended, at such fearful odds, should forever after be called by his name. The people of Charleston, with anxious and almost desponding hearts, watched the progress of that encounter from the wharves and house-tops of their City; and as the sun rose on the morning of the 29th of June upon the white and crescent-emblazoned flag of freedom, floating proudly from the parapet of the fort, while the ships of the defeated squadron were seen at distant anchorage, the shouts of rejoicing that rent the air were so loud and general and enthusiastic that no one there present would have dared to dream that within less than four generations that very place should be desecrated by notes of savage glee, sounded by a united and frantic populace over a dastardly attack upon the Government, for the building of which the intrepid Moultrie and his soldiers had hewn a corner stone.

Allusions were made to the battle of Great Meadows; and the fact that 107 years ago, on this day, George Washington marched out of Fort Necessity, relinquishing that important post to the French, after an encounter in which he taught the world a lesson in regard to American valor which they could not affect to overlook or forget.

He spoke of the remarkable and, as it would seem, Providential coincidence:—the death of the two great progenitors of the Declaration of Independence—John Adams and Thomas Jefferson, on the 4th of July, 1826.

Mr. Sumner then proceeded:—In a spirit of gratitude and veneration, we have briefly glanced at the Past.

We Live amid Stern and Tremendous Scenes!

The waves of our National Time, first troublous and ever surging with the storms, have for years with unexampled placidity or healthfulness of motion rolled down into the latitude of this generation.

One year ago to-day, the honest citizen whose mind was uneducated in the purposes of traitors saw nothing of desperate circumstance in the immediate future of our country. Party spirit was indeed stimulated to unprecedented extremities; the rancor and heartlessness of party strife disgusted every one who had not descended to the trade of a politician. But I undertake to say, neither North nor South were there any general apprehensions of the coming of events which we must now at least contemplate as stubborn facts, if we do not all of us deplore them as mournful realities.

Our fathers toiled up a rough ascent until they reached a fair table-land of freedom on the Mountain of Liberty. Their children for nearly a century have been in comparatively undisturbed enjoyment of unequaled political privileges. The hour has arrived for the testing of the strength of the beneficent civil institutions bequeathed to us; and, as I firmly believe, for our advance farther up the hights to new, bolder and more glorious governmental elevations.

My fellow citizens : I have not presumed to enter upon a review of the causes that brought about the struggle of the Revolution. A just and full-orbed synopsis of those causes would demand larger opportunity for preparing study for this occasion than I have enjoyed, more time for delivery than I could rightfully claim. But I do not deem myself in any degree incompetent to tell, within a space of startling brevity, the origin and the nature of the present Rebellion. The whole matter can be, in my judgment, related best with the employment of the simplest and most familiar idioms. It is true that for over thirty years elements of discord have been at work, on more than one occasion threatening our national overthrow or dissolution. At one time a violent outbreak, which promised disruption, was subdued by the indomitable will and executive hand of Andrew Jackson.

It has been prominently stated, and it is generally believed, that the disturbances of the present hour are the legitimate offspring of the theories of one man, long since passed away— in his speculations and plans embracing, perhaps, the thoughts and dispositions of the majority of the people of one state ; that John C. Calhoun, with his doctrine of Nullification, is the far-back but responsible author of this Rebellion. (A voice —" No, no.") I do not so think ; I beg leave to differ most thoroughly from that opinion. I know that there may instantly occur to the minds of many of my audience the quotations which the traitors of the day spread out in their publications from the writings of the high priest of Nullification. I will not declare that his logic may not oftentimes lead to dissolving views of the Union, even where such is not the open proclamation. But my belief remains, that had Calhoun, or such as he, never occupied a seat or uttered a sentiment in the Congress of our Republic the present rebellion would have developed. Of course, the so-called " President " of the so-called " Confederate States " and his co-traitors steal many of their apologetic ideas from the products of the wonderful intellect of Calhoun, the same as they steal the property of the Nation. It would be unnatural if they did not. They quote and steal Scripture for their purposes. But although the perversion in the latter case may be palpably flagrant, and the application in the former as plausibly apt and correct, I desire to submit some reasons which repose in the indisputable alphabet of modern history, why we should hold to the intrinsic originality of this insurrection with the persons who have it now in charge. And I shall be very brief.

In the first place, many causes are assigned by the same individuals as good in vindication of the conduct of the rebels, which are in themselves absolutely inconsistent. There is, in point of fact, no plain-faced logic in the manifestoes which are put forward from those quarters. The close and exhaustive analytical mind of Calhoun would have been mortified beyond measure and, as I must think, pained into abrupt and public rejection of the conflicting, nonsensical speech, denominated argument by its fulminators only, which we meet on the threshold of this discussion.

A general complaint is made, " The South has suffered at the hands of the North." In the same breath it is conceded and boasted that men with the most intense southern sympathies have thus far exercised predominating power in the administering of the laws of the government. The Chief Executive, the Senate, the Supreme Court have always promptly answered to their extreme demands. In what manner, then, has the South been oppressed by the North? Ask for specifications, and the ingenuity of intelligent and candid men is strained to its utmost tension in vain endeavors to gather from the vague and wild replies anything like a definite basis for this wholesale accusation. Many of our keenest and most unprejudiced statesmen have resolutely descended into this sea of inquiry, wrestling long and patiently for substantial answers, only to return to the open sky with their diving armor covered with the filth of abuse and vituperation. But we do know their reasons and object in this business. We will not seek their direct statements, for those are intended to conceal what their action pronounces.

Let us read History :—

The Rebels began their work of demoralization and disunion by affecting a very tender regard for the interests of Slavery. They ascribed to the North a desire to overturn that institution by direct interference in the domestic affairs of states. The charge was denied in terms so explicit, from authorities so potential, by actions so emphatic, as to leave no ground for decent repetition of the same charge. But the sound of this same accusation went up without ceasing or modification. The Senators and Representatives in Congress from the South who continued this peal of complaint knew that they were lying.

They desired that the compromise line of 1820 should no longer hinder them from making slave states north of the parallel therein prescribed. A majority of the Congressmen from the North objected to the breaking down of that consecrated wall of Freedom. They spoke not for "Northern Rights," but of the rights of Freedom. But as "Southern Rights" or the appetites of Slavery demanded, that compromise line was destroyed. The instruments in this nefarious plot were a weak Executive and corrupted Congressmen. It was "constitutionally" removed, through fraud; while they who attempted to maintain it in its integrity were denounced as sectional and fanatical, as worshipers of the negro. The men who launched forth these miserable and inapplicable epithets knew that they had achieved a great wrong by blatant pretense on the one hand and bribery on the other—that they were slandering good citizens and true—that they were attempting to hide their iniquity, their falsehood and treachery by a blackguard derision of patriots whom they could not wheedle nor frighten nor purchase into their scheme of wrong.

But the God of Nature was to prevent their entering the Territory of Kansas and devoting its soil to slavery. So they said when the Missouri Compromise was destroyed. Every representative of the peculiar institution who thus spoke, uttered a deliberate lie; for it was their intention, as afterward thoroughly manifested, to spread their system of African bondage over the wonderfully fertile lands thus opened to its blighting influences.

If they did believe that the God of nature would incline to ward out their beloved institution with uncompromising isothermal lines, they disclosed a profound moral obliquity by their desperate endeavors, in the face of such an acknowledgment and opinion, to force the shackled black man into Kansas, there to toil in competition with the white child of freedom. And if at the commencement of this nefarious work they were willing to confess that they were defying the God of Nature, they certainly concluded their abortive attempt with a new and compound name for the obstacle which they found in their path—New England Emigrant Aid Societies and Sharp's Rifles. While they said at the outset, with false tongues, It is foreordained of Heaven that Kansas shall be free; the Border Ruffians who were sent out by them on a voyage of practical inquiry and struggle in the premises returned with the answer, that whatever might be in the decrees of Providence concerning the future condition of the Territory, the laboring men of the North had overrun the land and would make good the prophecies of freedom for Kansas, which had been hypocritically mouthed by the masters in the slave oligarchy. And the burden of this report was partly taken up by the leading southern politicians. They exclaimed, "Alas! we are deprived of an accession to our slave-area on account of the villainous combination of Massachusetts men and Connecticut rifles." And for once, in this plain narrative, I am obliged to confess that they approximated to the truth. In place of a dove-like reverence for nature's accredited edict, they suddenly and philosophically rise to a white-heat hatred of New England gunpowder. There was much exaggeration even here. The freemen of the North were continually subject to insult, plunder and deadly attack, while the occurrence of retaliation and reparation was disproportionally rare.

Is it worth while to stop and mark the cluster of inconsistencies—to employ the mildest term—in this section of the record? First, the compromise line of 1820 is unfair and unjust in its cramping effects upon the South; a little farther on in the debate the talk is, Slave labor cannot be profitably employed north of the designated line—an assertion contradicted by the condition of Missouri and other border slave States; then upon the heels of the overthrow of the compromise comes a determined and unprincipled struggle in the Territory and in Congress to plant the institution of slavery in Kansas; then howling, and gnashing of teeth, threats of disunion because in a perfectly legitimate manner, and after the most outrageous attempts to render it otherwise, it was made evident that slavery would be crowded out of the land which is now represented as a free State by the last star on our banner.

John Brown—a man of three score, who went with peaceful intentions to Kansas, was there robbed and maltreated by the myrmidons of the slave oligarchy, there witnessed the murder of his son and the violation of his daughter by the scions of southern chivalry—in a fit of wild but methodical insanity contrived a plan for the wholesale emancipation of the slaves of northern Virginia. He succeeded in taking the United States arsenal at Harper's Ferry and scaring out the whole militia force of the Old Dominion. He was tried and condemned to be hung by the authorities of the State. And his offence was pronounced "Treason,"—among other titles. In spite of his acknowledged crimes, his conduct during his incarceration and at the place of execution was so manly and brave that he received openly expressed sympathy from thousands who did not and would not seek to detract from the measure of his guilt as pronounced by the court, or mitigate the severity of the penalty affixed thereto. The present rebels then asserted that the John Brown foray was a fair evidence of the temper and intentions of a majority of the northern people. That was a lie, and they knew it. It was uttered and harped upon principally for effect upon the ignorant masses beneath them, whom they were tutoring for the hard work of Treason. John Brown's trial informed every intelligent man at the North as to the condition of the social strata on which the slave States repose, and not only gave full play to the eccentric faculties of Governor Wise, but exhibited, as of singular species, the courage of the people of his commonwealth.

The Democratic party stood most ready, above all other political organizations, to conciliate the South. They seemed ready and anxious to go to any extent within the bounds of reason in promotion of the interests of their Southern brethren. I am not speaking as a partizan, or in any sense as a fault-finder; I state a fact. But the most prominent leader in this party refused at one period to comply with the demands of the slavocracy, and the latter would not permit his nomination for the presidency. The Democratic party was divided by the men who to-day are attempting the dissolution of the Union. By this division, alone, was the election of Stephen A. Douglas to the presidency prevented. It would be more difficult, if not impossible, to betray the uninformed populace into overt acts of treason if Douglas was chief executive. Some candid individuals among their number boldly confessed that this was the basis of their action at Baltimore.

It was said that the South desired new guarantees that slavery should not be interfered with in the states. Congress, at its last session, voted to place a clause in the Constitution which should recite this very assurance; and, had sober time permitted, all the free states would have ratified and sealed that clause. But this was not enough for the rebels. When this provision was formally asked for the Rebels hoped that it would be refused. When it was given they may have been somewhat disappointed, but their purpose was not changed.

During the last hours of the leaders of the Rebellion in the United States Senate and House of Representatives the talk of "Compromise" was long, tedious and extravagant. But through it all there are no reasonable grounds marked out by the secessionists on which they could rear a statement of provocations for anything approaching in character their present rebellious position. Some, indeed, who are now loudest in defence of the "Southern Confederacy," were then equally vehement in denouncing secession, painting its inevitable horrors in the most vivid colors.

The Secretary of War originally selected by President Buchanan, labored during his entire term of office in removing arms and war munitions from Northern manufactories and arsenals to Southern ports; causing, so far as he was able, the destruction of such implements of war remaining in the Northern states as he could not place to the direct advantage of the Traitors. The latest intelligence we have from this distinguished individual consists in a report of a balcony speech to a party of serenaders, in the course of which he incidentally remarks that he is "an honest man."

Abraham Lincoln of Illinois was, in November last, constitutionally elected President of these United States. It was so declared by John C. Breckenridge, in the United States Senate; at a time when several now prominent leaders of the Rebellion retained their seats in that body. It has been claimed that his election was just cause for a dissolution of the Union. To this assertion, Alexander H. Stephens, now Vice President of the "Confederate States" entered a formal and explicit denial. But that was some months ago, before Mr. Stephens had been bribed by a bauble office, and had ceased to speak the truth.

In his inaugural address, President Lincoln assured the people of the South that it was not within the possible intentions of his administration to interfere with their property in slaves; that, on the contrary, all their rights in this respect should be sacredly guarded. (A voice—"And he has not interfered with their peculiar institution.") As a venerable friend on my left suggests, the President has given uniform evidence of his purpose to fulfill that pledge. At the same time President Lincoln reminded the country that he had registered an oath in heaven to maintain the Government in its fullest integrity. He presumed that no citizen had sworn to aid in its overthrow. His announcement, however, that it was his intention as chief executive to hold and possess the public offices, the custom houses, dock yards, etc., belonging to the government, in the already rebellious states, was received throughout the South as a "Declaration of War!"

Now if any man wishes to go back still farther for first principles and underlying motives, I am content. But I can not go with him. I would not seek in the genius of Calhoun the beginning of this system of falsehood and organized treason. It may be a consolation to the prisoner at the bar, under indictment for murder, if he be allowed through counsel to refer to the fratricide of Abel, as recorded in the first chapters of Genesis; but the deliberations of the jury, I imagine, would still be confined to the relevancy and force of the testimony which they received from the witness stand.

The leaders of the present rebellion were determined to rule or ruin—to rule in the Union, or to rule over a fragment of the Union. They had, in their minds, a real cause for insurrection, not in the election of Mr. Lincoln but in the defeat of Mr. Breckenridge. The subtleties of Calhoun had no more educating influence over their actions than the essays of Seneca.

I shall not trace the history of this rebellion in anything like a detail rehearsal. The well-known character of its conductors would be sufficient to promise a record of infamy. At the head of the "Confederate States" stands Jefferson Davis, whose most prominent action heretofore has been the advocacy of the scheme of repudiating the state debt of Mississippi; a man noted for his licentiousness and his insufferable vanity; a man who has been denounced as a liar and a poltroon from one end of his state to the other, and who has not displayed even the " courage of the code " in resentment or vindication; a man over whose entire public life, clotted with selfish political intrigues, there have been cast no blessed shadows of repentance.

For his chief counsellor and " Attorney General "—his Sancho Panza—Mr. Davis employs one J. P. Benjamin, known and branded by his college tutors as a thief; while holding a seat in the U. S. Senate, recognized as the warm friend and special advocate of a nest of lobby corruptionists, whose rotten claims and gigantic land-bill swindles it was his function and delight to favor.

One of Mr. Davis' Secretaries illustrates his character by prophesying the occupation of Washington by the Rebels during the month of May—exhibiting at the moment of utterance a singular discretion, and, as time develops the truth of his prediction, marvellous gifts of prescience.

At the head of the Confederate troops is a General whose Virginia proclamation asserts that the President of the United States is an " abolitionist," the soldiers of the Government " hirelings," and the cry of the entire army of the Union, " Booty and Beauty !"

In their own chosen time the rebels proceeded to steal our forts and arsenals, our dock yards, depositories of money, custom-houses and public edifices of all descriptions, and to appropriate to their own use and aggrandizement all the National property which they could seize without immediate jeopardy of their precious lives. The hands of the Rulers of the Government seemed to be stayed from any effort to restrain them in their traitorous work. The administration of James Buchanan was partly involved in the Treason. The new President and his cabinet desired conciliation through kindness at the beginning of their rule ; and not until one month after the entrance of Mr. Lincoln and his advisers upon executive duties did it seem good or fit, in their eyes, to issue a proclamation of warning to the rebels, and calling upon loyal citizens to rally to the support of the Constitution and the laws.

And what was the immediate cause of that proclamation ?

On the 12th of April, 1861, the "Confederate forces" at Charleston opened a bombardment upon Fort Sumter. That Fort then contained less than seventy soldiers, including the officers, and they were sadly worn with protracted and exhausting labors and in a reduced condition both as respects supplies of provisions and ammunition. The reason assigned for the attack at that particular time was the discovered or revealed intention of the President to send a ship load of food to his starving soldiers, long confined on short rations within the walls of the fort. For this ostensible and assigned cause the traitors of the Rebellion of 1861 fired upon the Flag of the American Union. Up to that hour the people of the North watched their preparations with a quietness that seemed to betoken an almost supine indifference. The newspapers were covered with accounts of the threatening and formidable battery erections by the South Carolinians, and great interest was taken in the North in perusing those accounts; but more of anxiety was felt here respecting the possible organizations of treason at home, than concerning the things which the open-mouthed rebels at Charleston would dare to do. The intelligent strangers who were sojourning in our midst, and who gleaned all their impressions of our sentiments by surface views, did not hesitate to predict to their fellow citizens or subjects of other lands, the agreement on the part of the North to almost any terms for conciliation.

At the time the intelligence of the committing of this grand overt act reached the Federal Capital, I was in the city of Washington; and the first really confirmatory report of the facts which I gathered, were from the lips of an excited man, who, in front of one of the principal hotels, on Pennsylvania avenue, was engaged in relating the incidents of the bombardment as far as they had transpired, and denouncing the Rebels in unmeasured terms. That man was Stephen A. Douglas.

Up to this hour the traitors had proceeded with acknowledged and wonderful cunning. They had employed their subordinates at the North in the business of prating of peace by non-resistance, and shouting vociferously against the policy of coercion. Something of caution may be said to have been exhibited in their movements up to this point. Something like a shrewd regard for the position and influence of their helpmeets in the North appeared to exercise a modifying tone over their counsels and actions. But the blow now given was ordered in a crazy mood, and was a fatal one for the insurgents. The gun first fired at Sumter sounded the beginning of self-retributive folly. Few of us had ever seen the walls of the assaulted fort, but we all knew and loved and honored the flag of our Union. The heart of every loyal man was smitten with throes of indignation when that great insult was put upon our national ensign. The blood of every citizen was hot as his lungs drank in the very atmosphere of revengeful sorrow.

We all knew what that banner typified; what memories it could suggest from out its starry folds. We had seen its constellation growing larger with almost every alternate earthly revolution round the sun. Many of us had seen it on the high seas, streaming proudly over the deck of an American steamer. Or, on some beautiful moonlit night, in a comparatively quiet sea off the farther South American Cape, you may have witnessed, as I have, the hauling in sight of an English merchantman and a Boston clipper, their prows turned toward the same haven; and as the speaking-trumpet sounded hoarsely over the billows, you may have beheld the running up of our national ensign to the spanker peak in answer to the display of the cross of St. George; and experienced no small degree of enthusiasm and no light sense of national superiority, as the sharp-edged vessel of Yankee-land shook out her de gallants and royals, and flew away from the tardy keel of old England, leaving a wake of laughing waters behind her, while the flag of the Union whipped out its saucy stripes in the breeze. We may have seen it displayed from a sloop-of-war in a foreign harbor, its stripes falling gracefully in the lull of the wind below the upper deck port-holes, wrapping themselves partially, as in loving embrace, around the protruding muzzle of an eighty pound peacemaker. From the house-top of minister or consul it may have spoken to you in terms of cheering and protectful significance. We know that from every building of collected industry, from the tower of every church, college and academy in the land, for more than half a century it has been given to the winds. And there may be those among us who have seen, as we have all read, how it has flaunted on the field of battle; how it has been borne forward to the thickest of the fray with a determination and valor that could be paused only in death; how it has gleamed in the very spirit of exultation as after a desperate struggle it has been planted in triumph on the ramparts of the enemy. And you may have seen it, as on many a night I have delighted to behold it, waving over the superbly illuminated dome of the senate chamber or the hall of representatives at Washington; its ever unwinding folds bathed in a halo of upspringing light, playing upon the silver stars in its azure, which flashed with upturned faces as though responsive to signals from the glittering vault of heaven itself.

All our recollections of our country's history, all our desires for its future, have been cemented and harmonized by this beautiful expression of our National existence, power and glory. And it was upon this flag, floating peacefully over a fort built by our Government in Charleston harbor, for the protection there of American interests—a fort now garrisoned by less than seventy half-famished soldiers—it was upon this flag thus placed that these accursed traitors, these cowardly cut-throats dared to fire.

The people of the North had long borne the most flagrant insults from the sons of spurious " chivalry " in the South. Our time-honored and almost sainted customs were the habitual subject of their ridicule; our very industry and ingenuity was set down to the credit of sordid and avaricious impulse, by the lazy offspring of degenerate Virginia, themselves living on the National charity in sinecure offices at the Capital. Our religious ceremonies were intruded upon by their sneering and mockery; in hours of lowest debauchery they sought to cast upon our domestic altars the spawn of their vilest slander. All this had been endured without murmur or retort, in a spirit sometimes warming with contempt, but always philosophical and free from the nurture of retaliation in kind. But when this outrage was committed upon our Flag—fearful by all the circumstances connected with its perpetration—the candle of more than fraternal patience burned quick to the socket.

As we now reflect upon it, can we be surprised at the unanimity with which the people of the North called for measures of retribution? Do we stand amazed in view of the fact, that at the moment when this indignity was made known, party spirit, the great bane of the land, seemed overwhelmed and buried in a gushing wealth of patriotic sentiment? That from every hand, with inconsiderable and contemptible exceptions, the voice of our people was as the voice of one man for the vindication of the Government?

No! No! We cannot but feel: Never was there so wicked and wanton a Rebellion;—for never was there so kind and beneficent a government in all the earth, and never have the records of time produced a calendar containing the names and the deeds of such detestable wretches as are those who to-day imagine or pretend they rule in the land of slave auctions and cotton plantations.

The Nation—that portion of the Nation which has for many years constituted its chief strength and its undimmed glory, sprang to arms. The President's requisition for seventy-five thousand men was met, so far as readiness for service was concerned, in less than twenty-four hours after it had been given to the public.

And first and foremost in the field, were the sons of Massachusetts. O! Glorious old Commonwealth of Massachusetts! Thy Name had become a watch-word of Freedom in days long past. Now, thy vigilance, thy promptitude, thy sufferings and losses in the maintaining of the Union, of which thou hast ever been the crown jewel, has made thee doubly dear to the hearts of all thy children. It is with indescribable emotions of pride and joy that we remember we are on thy soil to-day. Thy sons hastened forth at their country's call, from the farm, the work-shop, the manufactory, the professional office, to re-consecrate, in the most impressive manner possible, the day of the battle of Lexington, and to render yet more "sacred" the soil of the Old Dominion..

I stood in the streets of the commercial metropolis as they marched through on their way to the Federal Capital. The scene presented was one of ovation. Right soldierly they kept on their line of march, their faces set like flint towards their posts of destination and danger. The impromptu and enthusiastic demonstrations along their route must have cheered and encouraged them, but these were not needed to stimulate their patriotic love and determination. They knew that they were about their Nation's business. On the following day we heard of their encounter in the city of Baltimore. In less than a week from that time I saw Massachusetts men reconstructing and guarding the railroad between Annapolis and Washington.

Nor, in this connection, should we neglect to acknowledge the ready and valuable services of that regiment from the Metropolis, composed of some of the worthiest and wealthiest young men of the city, who, leaving homes of cultivation and refinement and habits of life in the most exalted social circles, buckled on their armor at a day's warning, and in splendidly disciplined array, like the Old Guard of Napoleon, swept down the broad thoroughfare through crowds of weeping yet applauding relatives and friends, on their way to sustain their Massachusetts brethren, and to carve out for themselves enduring tablets of fame. All honor! all honor! to the flower of the American militia—the incomparable Seventh Regiment of New York.

Within three or four days from the issuing of the President's proclamation, the leading citizens of New York city irrespective of party, united in a call for a grand "Union Meeting," to be held in Union Square, on Saturday, the 20th of April. On the afternoon of that day, before the hour appointed for the meeting had arrived, the stores in the lower part of the city were closed, and people flocked to the place of assembling from all directions and in massive crowds. At the hour when the meeting was called to order, it was computed by careful estimators that not less than eighty thousand persons had ranged themselves within hearing distance of the speakers from the different stands. And the tide of attendance increased from that moment until the close of the ceremonies of the occasion. Never before, on this continent, was there such a gathering. Never were there so many elements, heretofore at complete political variance, brought in homogeneous contact, agreement and resolution. Upon the same platform were prominent citizens of all parties; and from their lips and hearts came burning words of patriotism. From those who, until a very recent period, had been the most noted champions of the "interest of the south," within the bounds of loyalty, the word was ardent and fierce—"We must drive the Traitors into the sea."

The merchant was there, pledging—I use the very language

of one of the most prominent among them—pledging "the commercial accomplishments of more than forty years hard labor over the counter and the ledger to the preservation of our Institutions and the sustaining of the Governmental authorities in the fullest and freest exercise of their constitutional prerogatives."

The Scotch citizen soldier was there, arrayed in the uniform of his highland regiment which had that evening received orders to prepare for the march to the Capital; through his leaders promising, if required, to march "through Baltimore or over the place where Baltimore once was."

The German citizen was there, patriotically addressing his brethren of like nativity in that same sweet accent which the Commander-in-chief of our army declared was most delightful to hear.

And the officers of the immortal sixty-ninth regiment—composed wholly of citizens of Irish extraction—were upon the platforms; relating substantial evidence of the faithfulness of their soldiers in this hour of trial; informing the assembled multitude that to fill a requirement for less than three hundred men, in that grand section of our army, over twenty thousand able-bodied Irishmen, thoroughly qualified for the most active and severe service, had pressed their claims for place, while the stations opened for recruits were still besieged by uncounted crowds. We knew that whatever of hesitation other classes of our foreign-born population might exhibit in presenting themselves in direct support of the Government, our elected rulers would find sufficient power at hand for the protection of their official residence and the ultimate execution of their mandates throughout the Union, among the adopted citizens from old Erin,—whose children "never turn their back to a foe in war or a friend in need." They knew what it was to live and suffer under an oppressive government; they appreciated the mildness and fostering care of our administrations.—And be it here remembered, when this regiment had entrenched themselves on the heights of Arlington, they planted their favorite battery-gun on their well-made embankment, and as it pointed traitor-ward, shotted to the lips, they called upon their Catholic Chaplain to baptize it in the name of Liberty and their holy religion.

The French citizen soldier was there ; proudly recounting the deeds of Lafayette, and swearing with a vivacity inimitable outside of his impetuous race, that he and his comrades would follow the teachings and examples of that loved companion of Washington, and if possible bear evidence that an equally unselfish impulse animated their hearts.

The exiled sons of Poland and Hungary were there; and their swarthy countenances grew livid with emotional expression as they spoke in language incoherent in itself, but unmistakable in its revelation of will, of Kosciusko, Kossuth and Anderson.

And those were there for whom it must have been equally unpleasant to behold and to be seen ; men who were compelled by the clearly-evinced purpose of the people to improve a last-grace opportunity of announcing their readiness to perform their share of labor in maintaining the Government in its integrity. There was Fernando Wood, long and universally recognized as the most unscrupulous demagogue, the most ambitious and reckless politician of the land,—who had but recently made a semi-official proposition to declare the " independence " of New York city as a new copy of the " model Dutch Republics." From the lofty eminence of prospective ruler over such a petty government, he suddenly tumbled down to the better place of tail-end and barely tolerated speaker at this mighty Union gathering.

Veterans who fought under our flag in the war of 1812 were there, clad in their well-worn yet well-preserved uniforms ; by their grave and venerable aspect, as well as by their occasional words of approbation, lending a solemn interest to the scene and deepening the resolutions of the younger members of the audience who were soon to start for the posts of danger and conflict.

And there were other persons and features in the scene whose presence was more august and exhilarating. Over the principal stand floated the parapet flag of Fort Sumter, which was nailed upon its staff, in the midst of the bombardment, by the daring Hart. And the extended hand of the bronze equestrian statue of Washington, rising from the center of the open square, grasped the shattered staff from which streamed the torn and perforated folds of that larger ensign which the brave garrison of less than seventy saluted, as they left their battered keep.

And there, by turns, on each of the platforms erected around the vast area, stood the heroes of the hour—the men who had lately won for themselves undying fame, while they had added a new and glorious chaplet to the brow of the Goddess of American Liberty. Major Anderson, Captains Doubleday and Foster were presented to those hosts of freemen, and received such patriotic cheer and homage as was never before paid to mortal men.

And while, again, we proclaim—Never before was there such an unprovoked and unrighteous rebellion, never such exhibitions of black-hearted ingratitude and treachery, we have now to add, with irrepressible and jubilant emphasis—Never was there such a spontaneous uprising of the people of a nation in support of the constitution and the laws.

At this mammoth Union meeting, it was agreed that the city of New York would "adopt" the families of the volunteers who there enlisted and proceeded to the seat of war. A "Union Defense Committee" was appointed, whose action from that date, it is fair and only just to say, has contributed as much to keep alive the military ambition and spirit of the people, and to promote the comfort of the soldiers, as any regularly organized commissary or sanitary department of the army. They first authoritatively informed the President and his cabinet of the endorsing and urging temper of the North. At this meeting there were subscribed by the merchant princes of New York and Brooklyn, to the fund for the equipment of volunteers and the maintenance of their families, over $100,000.

And as the sun commenced sinking behind the Elysian Fields, that immense assemblage sang in wonderful harmony, and with thrilling effect :

" When Treason's dark cloud hovers black o'er the land,
    And Traitors conspire to sully her glory,—
When that banner is torn by a fratricide band,
    Whose bright starry folds shine illumined in story,—
United we stand for the dear native land ;
For the Union we pledge every heart, every hand !
For the star-spangled banner in triumph shall wave
While the land of the free is the home of the brave."

From that hour to this, there has been no failing in the resolution and enthusiasm of the people. I need not recount the
events so ready in your recollection. An army of over two
hundred thousand men has been prepared for the field. More
than half that number are now in actual service. Men of great
distinction in civil life have left their ordinary professional pur-
suits to accept military commands.  BANCROFT LIBRARY

This day, a son and Ex-Governor of Massachusetts is engaged in the excellent work of arresting and endungeoning
the officially-clad traitors in that infernal nest of treason, the
City of Baltimore. From your own community men have
gone forth, eminently worthy to stand in the ranks of an army
on which the hope of the country reposes. From all New England the response to the Executive's call has been immediate
and hearty.

Little Rhode Island has sent forth large and superior forces,
which, with her youthful and intrepid Governor at their head,
have been appointed to posts of great honor and danger.

Connecticut has raised and dispatched a noble band of soldiers; like a careful mother, supplying them with every requisite of camp life and comfort.

The boys of Bennington have turned into service, in a manner creditable to the memories of their place; marching into
the front ranks with a step indicative of a like temper with
the Revolutionary Hero who declared, "The enemy is ours
to-night boys, or Molly Stark's a widow!"

And from the granite hills of New Hampshire and the pine
forests of Maine we have heard the tramp of serried and reso-
lute hosts.  Bancroft

The Empire State and the Key Stone State have more men
sworn into the U. S. service as volunteer soldiers than were
required by the proclamation of the 15th of April.

New Jersey raises four capital regiments, while her people
are praying for a larger requisition, and in their petition com-
plaining of a partiality toward sister loyal states.

As we turn our eyes to the West, what a spectacle is presented! In that quarter, the offer of men for the service far
exceeds any demand which the most apprehensive and timorous
in our cause have reason to anticipate. And to that region
we must look for a display of energetic military conduct, such

as the country particularly covets at this time. The fine audacity and quick execution of General Lyon and Colonel Blair provide some of the principal scenes in the gallery of war paintings which this contest thus far has afforded.

Although there has been no great battle, there are many noble dead to mourn. Brethren peculiarly our own, children of the old Bay State, Needham, Whitney and Ladd, —they have been stricken down by assassins in a city which has no monument within its limits equal to that which shall be erected to their honor. Our sorrow for those who have fallen in this rebellion shall be the regret of men who expect in part to witness and wholly to anticipate their exceeding great reward. And on this day, in this quiet village, as sinks the sun behind yon pleasant hill, we will commence for ourselves the tribute of acknowledgment and praise while we mention the names of the imperial Vosburgh, the accomplished Winthrop, the brave and skillful Greble, the chivalrous Ellsworth! They have been laid in their final resting place, wrapped in the flag they died to defend. Their deeds are things tangible in the memories of all patriots; and in time to come where thousands now weep over their fate, millions shall pronounce their names in grateful and immortal song.

From a too intense apprehension in regard to our immediate future, as it might be shaped by the conduct of those engaged in the administering of national affairs, our attention has been frequently diverted to an inquiry as to the views which other governments have chosen to take of our condition and prospects. And here, to the majority of our people, there has been food for the profoundest wonder.

The English government has professed the utmost detestation of African slavery. Notwithstanding the universally known and acknowledged fact that the English forced this system of bondage upon unwilling and protesting Colonists, for the purpose of her own aggrandizement, she has been for years in the habit of sniveling over what she termed the inconsistences in our civil creed and our institutions. I think it cannot be fairly denied that she has occupied a moral vantage ground in this particular; that she has been, despite all the unpleasant incidents in our connection with her, entitled by her one great act of Emancipation to the privilege of reading homilies to all other nations on the wickedness of human slavery. Nor has her right in these matters been largely questioned. Some of us have been glad to peruse the elaborate addresses of her Exeter Hall Committees and her African Civilization Societies, and have pointed with a liberal pride to her position on the agitating question of our own land. If it be said that all these expressions of sentiment were informal, were not the voice of the Government, it is an easy and full reply to say that the chief counselors of the Kingdom condescended to participate in such expressions, and to give the italicising force of their names to the phillipics which the British public have pronounced against the masters of slaves in the South and their peculiar friends in the North. They have not failed to receive biting retorts in the fashion of reminders—that the staple for their principal manufactories was planted, cultivated, gathered and made ready for their eager market by the hands of enslaved toil. But either by the most discreet silence or by an Edinburgh essay on their irresponsibility for the character of remote sources of raw material, they have escaped much opprobrium, as well as laid perfectly dormant their sensitive conscience. But the hour that tests our love for and fidelity to the Union weighs in the balance their professions of moral and christian sentiment bearing upon the question of African Slavery, and proves them miserably lacking.

From the moment when this Rebellion assumed formidable proportions, the proposition to recognize the " Southern Confederacy " was heard in the English Parliament. Indeed, from the quickness and persistency exhibited in pressing this motion reason was given for suspecting that there was a direct collision between members of the House of Commons, especially representing British manufactory interests, and the Usurpers of the South.

The leading press of the Kingdom—by no means bound by the cotton lords of the land—has continually mocked our tribulations, and sung the praises of the chiefs of Treason. At one time it represented our government as never strong, and about to fall in pieces. It has proceeded to accuse the people of these Northern States with blood-thirstiness, as soon as we evinced a determination to support the Constitution in its integrity, and insist upon the execution of the laws. With an exhibition of Egyptian ignorance concerning our geographical, political, industrial and moral positions, it has sought to secure the acknowledgment at home of the " Southern Confederacy," and respect for the rebels throughout other nations to whom it spoke in somewhat official tones. Such a fearful want of correct information, or such reckless disregard for the simple truths of our condition was made manifest by the first print of the Kingdom, that we could not expect a very wise and cordial support in the sentiment of the masses to whom it practically dictated.

It may be said that we are yet in doubt as to what the final action of Great Britian may be. Instead of relieving, this fact serves to aggravate her permanently despicable position in our eyes. And it should be proclaimed, that the loyal people of these United States are rapidly losing sentiments of regret at the equivocal view which the English Government manifests towards us, in poorly concealed hopes that she may be induced in her mercenary greed to extend an arm of positive help to the rebellious foe.

The fact is, my fellow citizens, Canada is inconveniently ruled at present. We have not employment for a tithe of the fighting material that is chafing for military exploits. Our landlords have long declared that the other side of the Niagara was very much needed for the extension of a favorite watering-place. And upon the western shore there is a beautiful little Island, called " Vancouver," which the Californians, with their proverbial filibustering spirit, have long regarded with fretful vision. If the inhabitants of the British possessions immediately attached or contiguous to our territory, feel disposed at any moment to act a little on the " independent "—as without a great deal of encouragement on our part it is well known they would—we shall be probably induced to take such a " neutral stand " as will afford them perhaps more than an even opportunity to throw off the yoke of the " shop-keepers' sovereign."

The position of France is certainly favorable. The Emperor explicitly recognizes the Southern Confederacy in the only manner in which it deserves recognition; and by his rules respecting the entrance of their vessels into his ports, he has indicated that he will have no alliance or affiliation with the traitors.

The noble heroes of Italy seem to be reclining on their arms in silent yet disciplining study of our action. A new bond of sympathy has been forged between us. Not through the traditions of the past, but by the realities of the present, do we speak together. With what profound interest must they read the intelligence of the progress of our struggles. They can not be wrong in their judgment as to which side of the contest should seize the sympathies of a people who have recently cast off, or who are about to unloose for themselves, the manacles of tyranny.

The Congress of the United States, in accordance with a special call of the President, meets this day to ratify the action of the President within the past few months, and to devise means for carrying on the work of trampling this rebellion under foot. For no other purpose was it called. With the feeblest respect for the wishes of the people, it can entertain no other or different propositions. The bare idea of compromise with the rebels is so revolting to the patriot that it would seem past the audacity or weakness of any sane man to suggest it in the Capital counsels. We feel assured that there will be no temporizing with the traitors; but that this very time will have been rendered more memorable and sacred by the initiatory labor of the extraordinary Congress which assembles to-day. God grant that it may be so.

Our Federal Capital is safe. Over seventy thousand troops surround it in sentinel array. On the Virginia Bank, from the Falls of the Potomac down to the Hights of Arlington, and reaching to eminences overlooking the very shades of Mount Vernon, there is one continuous line of thinking bayonets, whose burnished blades echo back to the Blue Ridge the fires of the evening sun.

In a large room in an ancient building devoted to the Department of War, at Washington, is seated a venerable old man, matured and grown gray in the service of this country. To him all eyes are turned; all ears are open to catch his word of command. The majesty of his presence and power is unequaled in the world ; for he points the rifles, and plants and sights the artillery of FREEDOM.

There are local associations which might be revived to-day. One hundred years ago to-day the anniversary of the Declaration of Independence was celebrated for the first time by the inhabitants of the organized town of Great Barrington—the corporate existence of this town dating from the 30th of June preceding. But all local associations are swallowed up in the great thought of our Nationality. Give another hour to their review ; now render them humbly subservient to the supreme consideration of our common country.

We stand here to-day, first recognizing the glorious truth of our citizenship in a Republic unequaled in its expanse of territory, unapproachable throughout the world's history in the freedom and beneficence of its institutions. And if I might do so with pardonable egotism, I would desire to borrow something of impressive significance, while at the same time I gather a shadow of apology for what otherwise might be deemed a naked impertinence in my position, by reminding you that those who have had the order of this Celebration in charge have seen fit, with very brief notice, to call for an address from one of your sons whose place is not now amongst you, whose home is upon the shore of another ocean, and yet whose proudest boast remains, that although thousands of miles measure the distance between his adopted residence and these grand old mountains and this beautiful valley, he could not there be anything other or less than an American citizen.

Thank God ! the appreciation of our equal national brotherhood grows brighter and more beautiful in the tempest. We are a broadly-built, a widely settled people, living under one embracing government.

The winter sun that rises from the surging Atlantic upon the cold and austere coast of New England, sweeps grandly over the bosom of a mighty continent, to find its billowy resting-place in the calm waters of the Pacific, and in its setting hour, to pour through the Golden Gate upon a people of the same great Nation a magnificent Benediction of Heavenly Light. You may catch glimpses of his beams early on your new year's morning, as surrounded by a train of clouds, which he has lifted from the Atlantic and from your rivers and lakes; day by day, in collusion with prevailing winds, he draws them farther and farther West, on his veiled but royal march across the plains, until with increasing seductive influence he rolls them over the snow-capped summits of the Sierra Nevadas— then touching with warmer rays the spray of the Pacific, he thence evokes a greeting procession of vapors, which meeting and mingling with the mists of the East, above the uttermost parts of our land, are there at last broken in genial and baptismal showers. Nature, with all her inarticulate voices—the wheeling apparatus of our planetary system—the ever shifting and healthful play of the chemistry of air—the geography of a hemisphere—the embracing tides of oceans—the flowing of streams—the basoning of lakes—the granite girding of huge mountains, whose peaks spring into regions of ethereal chastity, there everlastingly crowned with frosts of saintliness which testify to all the land the blessedness of the summer seasons, as they melt and trickle down the hoary cliffs in fertilizing tears of joy—the variegated landscape of vast, luxuriant and chaining valleys—the ripening under the same parallel, in different longitudes, of temperate and tropical fruits—the telegraphic whisperings of the leaves of tender shrubbery and stalwart forest monarchs—the flying eddies of desert sands— the smiling into richest fragrance and most bewitching beauty of countless wild flowers, gathered into new, representative and sisterly clusters by the traveler who journeys from sea to sea—all, all unite in unceasing sacramental office of re-marrying this beloved people in one undivided, indissoluble Nation.

Fellow citizens, the hour is full of instruction, and not devoid of cheer. The lessons are plain, and the hopes which it inspires are generous and holy.

We are assured of the inherent strength of our Government above our highest anticipations of old. No weakness in the Executive office, no cowardice and political chambering on the part of the leading counselor in the chair of state, no disasters on the field of skirmish, brought about through the incompetency of Brigadier-Generals illegitimately promoted from obscure private life to important military commands,— none of these can have a permanently injurious effect upon our cause. Of men and money, of arms and provisions, we have an abundance; and let those challenge our wrath who think such action pleasant or safe.

But remember, in the maintaining of this government, at this crisis, we all have a part to perform. Our part may be a very humble one but, whatever it be, as patriotic citizens we must contribute with all our energy and soul. Of our means, of our influence, of our heart's blood it may be, something is required. Let it be given freely, with the prayer that all these sacrifices and endeavors in behalf of the kindest and most enlightened rule the world has ever known, may speedily, by the people of a regenerate and peaceful nation, be laid as an acceptable votive offering at the footstool of the God of a Christian Civilization.

www.ingramcontent.com/pod-product-compliance
Lightning Source LLC
Chambersburg PA
CBHW061239260626
47172CB00003B/930